丁丁企鵝遊學館

閱亮點
ENRICH SPOT

丁丁企鵝遊學館

有啥情有七竟學英語

03 外出篇 Outing

原作 江記 · 撰文 閱亮點編輯室

Contents
目錄

Meet the characters   6
角色介紹

Greeting someone   8
問候

Running into a friend   9
碰見朋友

The bakery   10
餅店

Crossing the road   11
過馬路 ① ②

Taking the escalator   13
乘扶手電梯

The park   14
公園

The swings   15
秋千

The merry-go-round   16
氹氹轉

The beach   17
沙灘 ① ②

The sea is polluted...   19
海水變污水了……

The swimming pool   20
游泳池

Going hiking   21
遠足

Going camping   22
露營

Having a picnic 23
野餐

The library 24
圖書館

Going grocery shopping 25
買東西

The checkout 26
收銀處

The ice cream truck 27
雪糕車

Eating out 28
在外吃飯

The Chinese restaurant 29
茶樓

The railway station 30
鐵路站 ① ②

Taking the train 32
乘鐵路

Taking the tram 33
乘電車

Taking the ferry 34
乘渡輪

The bus stop 35
巴士站 ① ②

Taking the bus 37
乘巴士

Ding Ding is on the phone! 38
打電話，聊聊天！

Meet the characters
角色介紹

Ding Ding
A little penguin.
He is a lively kid
who is ready to play
at all times!

Mum
Ding Ding's mother.
She always teaches
Ding Ding to be
a well-behaved child.

Dad
Ding Ding's father.
He loves his family
so much.

Mushroom

A friend of Ding Ding.
Her hairstyle makes her
look like a mushroom!

Glasses

Another friend.
He always wears
a pair of glasses.

Ryan

Ding Ding's cousin.
He is a mature penguin
for his age.

Masihung

A bear who wears a mask on his face.
He goes beyond lazy and
into super lazy!

Panda

A roommate of Masihung.
He is a conscientious panda. Sadly,
he is worlds apart from Masihung.

⚪ Greeting someone 問候

1️⃣ Hi there. 你好。

2️⃣ What's new? 你好嗎？

3️⃣ Good to see you! 很開心見到你！

4️⃣ How's it going? 最近好嗎？

Running into a friend
碰見朋友

1 Catch you later. 稍後見。　　2 See you. 再見。

What can we get at the bakery?

1 Burger

2 Sandwiches

3 Bread

Someone is sneaking a taste!

1 Skip 跳

2 Zebra crossing 斑馬線

3 Dangerous 危險

4 Get hurt 受傷

1 Blush 臉紅

2 I'm bursting! 我很想上廁所！

3 Wait 等待

Taking the escalator
乘扶手電梯

1 Oops! 哎呀！（在發生小意外時說）　**2** Watch your step. 走路要小心。

3 Lose your balance 失平衡

The park 公園

1 Hang on. 等一下。

2 Snack 點心

3 Come on. 快來吧。

4 Together 一起

1 Swing 盪秋千

2 Fall off 從（秋千）上掉下來

The merry-go-round 氹氹轉

1 Vast 寬闊

2 Swim ring 泳圈

3 Bring along 攜帶

1 Sandcastle 沙堡壘

2 Collect 收集

3 Seashell 貝殼

4 Instead 寧願（做另一件事）

The sea is polluted...
海水變污水了……

1 Polluted 受污染

2 Ever again 在未來任何時候

3 Protect 保護

The swimming pool 游泳池

1 Hold their breath 憋氣

2 Make a face 扮鬼臉

Going hiking 遠足

I'm following the trail to go up the mountain.

Wahoo!
Hiking jokes are hill-arious!

1 Trail　山路

2 Hilarious　很好笑

Going camping 露營

1 Especially 尤其

2 Friend 朋友

3 Cool 涼快 / 帥氣

Having a picnic 野餐

1 Weather 天氣

2 Tomorrow 明天

3 Cheers! 乾杯！

4 Enjoy! 好好享用吧！

The library 圖書館

1 Pick 挑選

2 Borrow 借入

3 Shush! 噓！（安靜點）

Going grocery shopping 買東西

1 Grocery 食品和日用品

2 Goodies 好東西

3 You've freaked me out! 你嚇壞我了！

The checkout 收銀處

1 Scan 掃描

2 Point rewards card 積分卡

The ice cream truck 雪糕車

1. Chocolate 朱古力

2. Coconut 椰子

3. Strawberry 草莓

Eating out 在外吃飯

1 Fidget 動來動去

2 Slurp 咕嚕咕嚕地喝

3 Where are your manners? 你這樣很失禮儀。

The Chinese restaurant 茶樓

1 Shrimp dumpling 蝦餃

2 Spring roll 春卷

3 Shumai 燒賣

4 Egg tart 蛋撻

We're going to take the train today. Let's get the tickets!

I'm good. I have a travel card, but I need to top it up.

1 Ticket 車票

2 I'm good. 不用了。

3 Top up 增值

The railway station 鐵路站 ②

1 Remember 記得

2 Tap 拍（卡）

Taking the train 乘鐵路

1 Get off 下車

2 Count me too! 也算上我吧！

32

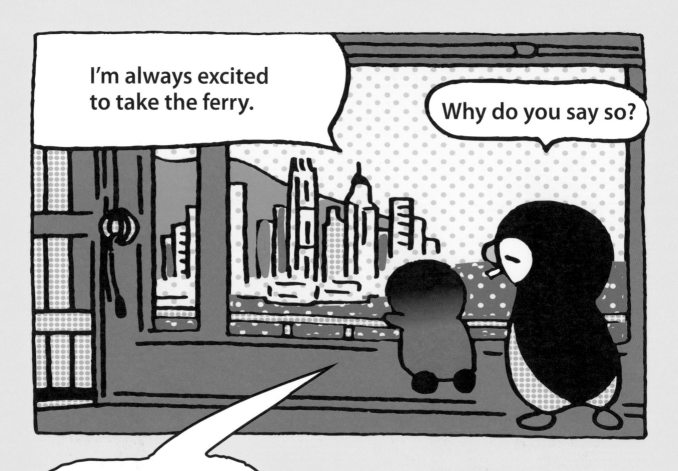

I'm always excited to take the ferry.

Why do you say so?

Because I might see a whale swimming nearby!

The bus stop 巴士站 ①

Mum, hurry up!
The bus stop is over there.

How often does the bus come?

It comes every 30 minutes.
He must have missed the bus.

Murmur

OH!

Poor guy!

How sad...

❶ Hurry up 快點

❷ Murmur 低聲說

The bus stop 巴士站 ②

1 Excuse me. 打擾一下。

2 Sorry? (I don't understand) 這裏解作「你說什麼?我不太明白。」

1 Crowded 擠逼

2 Chug 引擎隆隆的聲音

Ding Ding is on the phone!
打電話，聊聊天！

丁丁企鵝遊學館

有情有境學英語 03 外出篇 Outing

原作	江記（江康泉）
撰文	閱亮點編輯室
內容總監	曾玉英
責任編輯	Zeny Lam & Hockey Yeung
顧問編輯	Catherine Chan & Kevin Chu
書籍設計	Stephen Chan

出版	閱亮點有限公司 Enrich Spot Limited
	九龍觀塘鴻圖道 78 號 17 樓 A 室
發行	天窗出版社有限公司 Enrich Publishing Ltd.
	九龍觀塘鴻圖道 78 號 17 樓 A 室
電話	(852) 2793 5678
傳真	(852) 2793 5030
網址	www.enrichculture.com
電郵	info@enrichculture.com
出版日期	2021 年 7 月初版

承印	嘉昱有限公司
	九龍新蒲崗大有街 26-28 號天虹大廈 7 字樓

定價	港幣 $88　新台幣 $440
國際書號	978-988-75704-0-0
圖書分類	(1) 兒童圖書　　(2) 英語學習

DING DING

ding_ding_penguin